**CHECK FOR
AUDIO CD IN
FRONT OF BOOK**

Replacement costs will be
billed after 42 days overdue.

Dear Parents & Teachers,

Teachers and parents agree that children are motivated to learn when the process is meaningful and enjoyable. It is upon this principle that *Phonics Songs* is based.

Children build confidence in their skills as they blend consonant sounds and long vowel word families that are set to catchy melodies and amusing lyrics. *Phonics Songs* will promote learning a sight word vocabulary and encourage children to practice decoding words.

Modalities such as auditory, visual and tactile modes are used in this approach. Every type of learner has a chance to succeed with the *Phonics Songs*. Use *Phonics Songs* to help your children build a solid foundation for reading.

Felice Green, Ed.M.

CREDITS

Executive Producer: Felice Green
Producer: Robert Sands
Lyrics: Felice Green, Janet Scarloff and Robert Sands
Music: Robert Sands
Vocals: Janet Sclaroff, Barbara Sommers and Lou Ann Heth
Recorded at Wallaee, Inc. and Windmill Studio
Engineer: Paul Grosso and Mike Lowinski
Cover Design: Darcy Frachella / Imaginaction
Layout: Thalia DeLong and Michelle Hagy/ Imaginaction
Illustrators: Mark Cottell, Michelle Hagy and Mark Kauffman

Suggestions for use

As children progress through *More Phonics Songs*, they gradually take on more and more responsibility for their learning. For example, each song has two verses. In the second verse, words have been omitted from the tape. The children are asked to read these words independently. The following suggestions will help you in making the most of this book and its activities.

1. MOTIVATE
Use the song to motivate the learner to want to know more about the word family. Let the child sing along with or without a lyric sheet.

2. DIRECT
Explain what a word family is and go over the phonic sounds individually. Ask the children to name other words with similar sounds. The script, which is provided on page three, will help you explain word families and sounds.

3. PRACTICE
Do the practice example together. Let the children make up some of their own drawings. Encourage proper pronunciation and handwriting.

4. REINFORCE / ENRICH
Allow children to listen to the tape and do the activity again as they follow along with the voice on the tape. Repeating this step will not only improve retention, but it can be fun. Enrich your activities by having the children make rhyming books or by playing concentration with word family matches.

This is an example of the script using the **ay** family. It can be modified by replacing any of the boldface words with the correct words from another word family. If you have any questions you can listen to the tape for guidance.

Hello boys and girls. We are going to learn some new words. These new words are all part of a special family called a word family. Point to the a-y in the roof of the house. A-y says *ay*. The *ay* family lives in this house. Put your finger on the letter s which is outside of the house. The letter s makes the *s* sound. Let's say the *s* sound as we move our finger along the path into the ay family house. Ready? Here we go, *s-ay*, **say**! We just made a word, say. s-a-y.

Put your finger on the letter r which is outside of the house. The letter r makes the *r* sound. Let's say the r sound as we move our finger along the path into the ay family house. Ready? Here we go, *r-ay*, **ray**! We just made a word, ray. r-a-y.

The words day and pay are also in the *ay* family house.

Now let's sing a song using these words.

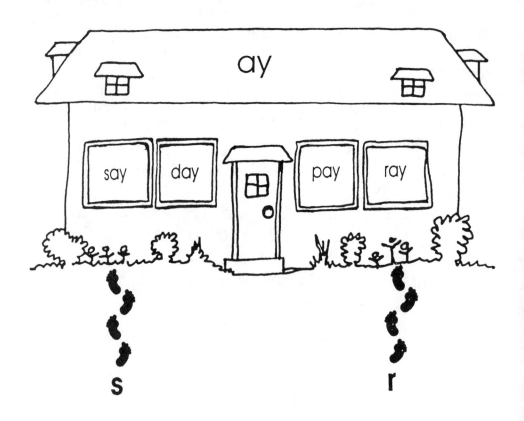

ay

say | day | pay | ray

s   r

* *

Follow the path to make words in the **ay** family. Write the word on the line.

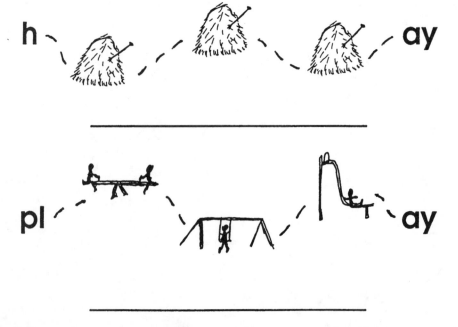

h ~ ~ ~ ~ ~ **ay**

_____

pl ~ ~ ~ ~ ~ **ay**

_____

AY

The letters a-y,
They always say *ay*.
Just like in the words
Day and way,
Say and pay,
And hay and ray.

The letters a-y,
They always say *ay*.

D says *d*.
Put *d* before *ay*.
D-ay always says day.

S says *s*.
Put *s* before *ay*.
S-ay always says say.

Well, w says *w*.
Put *w* before *ay*.
W-ay always says way.

Now let's use
Some of these new words
In a silly song
That you have never
    heard.

What can I say
On this gray day.
I just want to play.
But is there any way?
There's no sun ray.
To light up the day.
I guess I'd have to say

That I don't like gray.

Now YOU can say
The words with *ay*
When we sing
About this gray day.

What can I **say**
On this gray **day**.
I just want to **play**.
But is there any **way?**
There's no sun **ray**.
To light up the **day**
I guess I'll have to **say**
That I don't like **gray**.

Now remember, the let-
    ters a-y
Always say *ay*.
Just think of the story
Of this gray day.

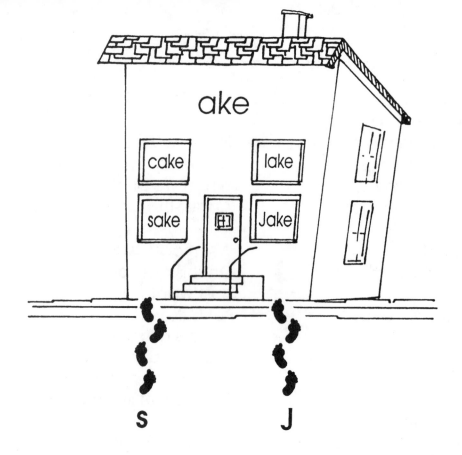

ake

cake   lake

sake   Jake

s   J

* *

Follow the path to make words in the **ake**
family. Write the word on the line.

r   **ake**

_____

c   **ake**

_____

AKE

The letters a-k-e,
They always say *ake*.
Just like in the words
Rake and Jake,
Lake and sake,
And cake and take.

The letters a-k-e,
They always say *ake*.

T says *t*.
Put *t* before *ake*.
T-ake always says take.

C says *c*.
Put *c* before *ake*.
C-ake always says cake.

Well, s says *s*.
Put *s* before *ake*.
S-ake always says sake.

Now let's use
Some of these new words
In a silly song
That you have never

heard.

Did you take the rake
From mean old Uncle
 Jake?
Oh, for goodness sake
Did you make a mistake.
He's fishing by the lake.
And to him you will take
A chocolate pudding
 cake.
That I must quickly bake.

Now YOU can say
The words with *ake*
When we sing
About mean old Uncle
 Jake.

Did you take the **rake**
From mean old uncle
 Jake?
Oh, for goodness **sake**
Did you make a **mistake**?
He's fishing by the **lake**.
And to him you will **take**
A chocolate pudding
 cake
That I must quickly **bake**.

Now remember, the let-
 ters a-k-e
Always say *ake*.
Just think of the story
Of mean old Uncle Jake.

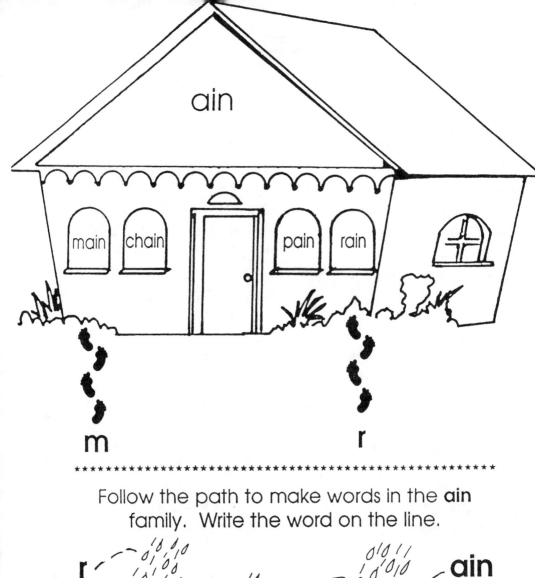

ain

main chain pain rain

m   r

* *

Follow the path to make words in the **ain** family. Write the word on the line.

r $\dashrightarrow$ **ain**

_____

ch $\dashrightarrow$ **ain**

_____

AIN

The letters a-i-n,
They always say *ain*
Just like in the words
Rain and chain
Grain and train
And brain and pain.

The letters a-i-n,
They always say *ain*

R says *r*.
Put *r* before *ain*.
R-*ain* always says rain.

M says *m*.
Put *m* before *ain*.
M-*ain* always says main.

Ch says *ch*.
Put *ch* before *ain*.
Ch-*ain* always says chain.

Now let's use
Some of these
new words,
In a silly song
That you have
never heard.

From the dark
domain
With bolts from his
brain,
Through the
driving rain

And carrying a chain
He headed towards a
train
That stopped at 5th and
Main
To sing his last refrain
From the dark domain.

Now YOU can say
The word with *ain*
When we sing
About the dark domain.

From the dark **domain**
With bolts from his **brain**
Through the driving **rain**
And carrying a **chain**
Heading towards a **train**
That stopped at 5th and
Main
To sing his last
refrain
From the dark
domain.

Now remember
the letters a-i-n
Always say *ain*
Just think of the
story
Of the dark
domain.

- 9 -

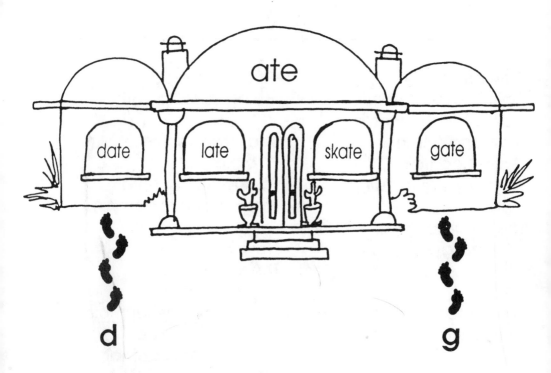

ate

date   late   skate   gate

d   g

* *

Follow the path to make words in the **ate**
family. Write the word on the line.

pl  ate

_____

g 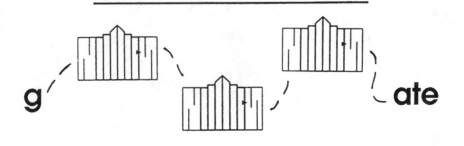 ate

_____

ATE

The letters a-t-e,
They always say *ate*.
Just like in the words
Date and late,
Fate and gate,
And skate and plate.

The letters a-t-e
They always say *ate*.

D says *d*.
Put *d* before *ate*.
D-ate always says date.

G says *g*.
Put *g* before *ate*.
G-ate always says gate.

Now, s-k says *sk*.
Put *sk* before *ate*.
Sk-ate always says skate.

Now let's use
Some of these new words

In a silly song
That you have never
    heard.

I had a date
To go out for a skate.
My mate was late
And then they closed the
    gate.
So we didn't skate.
Maybe it's my fate
To have a late night date
And never ever skate.

Now YOU can say
The words with *ate*
When we sing
About the late night date.

I had a **date**
To go out for a **skate**.
My mate was **late**
And they closed the **gate**.
So we didn't **skate**.
Maybe it's my **fate**.
To have a late night **date**
And never ever **skate**.

Now remember, the let-
    ters a-t-e
Always say *ate*.
Just think of the story
About the late night date.

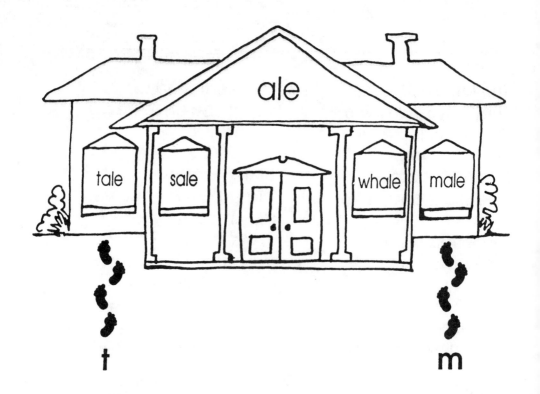

ale

tale sale whale male

t m

* *

Follow the path to make words in the **ale** family. Write the word on the dotted line.

wh ale

_____

sc ale

_____

ALE

The letters a-l-e,
They always say *ale*.
Just like in the words
Pale and whale,
Tale and Yale,
And scale and male.

The letters a-l-e,
They always say *ale*.

T says *t*.
Put *t* before *ale*.
T-ale always says tale.

P says *p*.
Put *p* before *ale*.
P-ale always says pale.

Now, *y* says *y*.
Put *y* before *ale*.
Y-ale always says Yale.
Now let's use
Some of these new words

In a silly song
That you have never
    heard.

I like the tale
About the little whale,
Who was the first male
To go to Yale.
He bought clothes on
    sale,
But his face went pale
When he broke the scale
Near that female whale.

Now YOU can say
    The words with *ale*
When we sing
About the little whale.

I like the **tale**
About the little **whale,**
Who was the first **male**
To go to **Yale.**
He bought clothes on
sales.
But his face went **pale**
When he broke the **scale**
Near that female **whale.**

Now remember, the letters
    a-l-e
Always say *ale*.
Just think of the story
About the little whale.

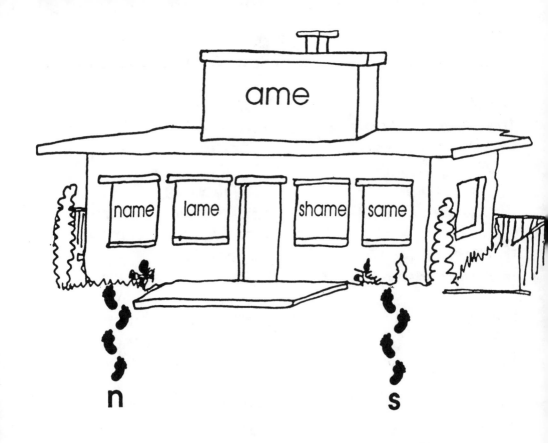

****

Follow the path to make words in the **ame** family. Write the word on the line.

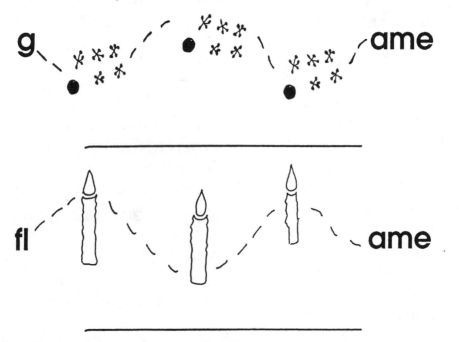

g   **ame**

_____

fl   **ame**

_____

AME

The letters a-m-e,
They always say *ame*.
Just like in the words
Name and game
Same and blame
And lame and shame.

The letters a-m-e,
They always say *ame*.

N says *n*.
Put *n* before *ame*.
N-*ame* always says name.

S says *s*.
Put *s* before *ame*.
S-*ame* always says same.

S-h says *sh*.
Put *sh* before *ame*.
Sh-*ame* always says
    shame.

Now let's use
Some of these new words
In a silly song
That you have never
    heard.

Isn't it a shame
That I don't know your
    name?
My excuse is lame.
But I can't take the
    blame.

I had an old flame.
And you look just the
    same.
Isn't it a shame
That I call you by his
    name?

Now YOU can say
The words with *ame*
When we sing
About my old flame.

Isn't it a **shame**
That I don't know your
    name?
My excuse is **lame**.
But I can't take the
    blame.
I had an old **flame.**
And you look just the
    same.
Isn't it a **shame**
That I call you by his
    name?

Now remember, the
    letters a-m-e
Always say *ame*.
Just think of the story
About my old flame.

eat

heat seat treat beat

h   b

Follow the path to make words in the **eat** family. Write the word on the line.

tr — eat

_____

b — eat

_____

EAT

The letters e-a-t,
They always say *eat*.
Just like in the words
Beat and neat,
Treat and meat,
And seat and wheat.

The letters e-a-t,
They always say *eat*.

B says *b*.
Put *b* before *eat*.
B-eat always says beat.

S says *s*.
Put *s* before *eat*.
S-eat always says seat.

Well, h says *h*.
Put *h* before *eat*.
H-eat always says heat.

Now let's use
Some of these new words,
In a silly song
That you have never
  heard.

Listen to the beat.
It sounds kind of neat.
But to play in all this heat
Is really quite a feat.
He sits upon his seat
And plays a steady beat.
He deserves a treat,

Just to play in all the heat.

Now YOU can say
The words with *eat*
When we sing about
Playing in the heat.

Listen to the **beat**.
It sounds kind of **neat**,
But to play in all the **heat**
Is really quite a **feat**.
He sits upon his **seat**
And plays a steady **beat**
He deserves a **treat**,
Just to play in all the **heat**.

Now remember, the
  letters e-a-t
Always say *eat*
Just think of the story
About playing in the heat.

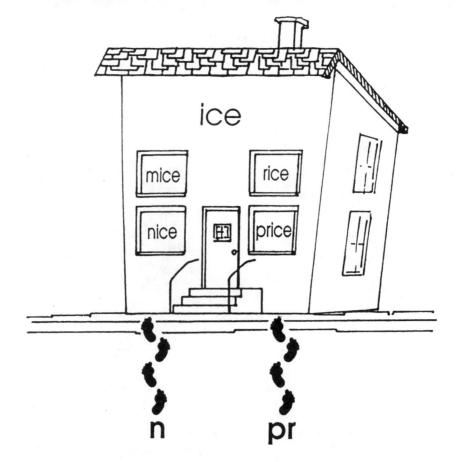

ice

mice   rice

nice   price

n   pr

****

Follow the path to make words in the **ice**
family. Write the word on the line.

d   **ice**

_____

pr   **ice**

_____

ICE

The letters i-c-e,
They always say *ice*.
Just like in the words
Rice and dice,
Twice and mice,
And price and nice.

The letters i-c-e,
They always say *ice*.

R says *r*.
Put *r* before *ice*.
R-ice always says rice.

T-w says *tw*.
Put *tw* before *ice*.
Tw-ice always says twice.

Well, d says *d*.
Put *d* before *ice*.
D-ice always says dice.

Now let's use
Some of these new words,

In a silly song
That you have never
   heard.

I told you twice.
It isn't very nice.
And you'll pay the price
If you don't eat your rice.
It isn't very nice,
To leave it for the mice.
You'll pay the price
If you don't eat your rice.

Now YOU can say
The words with *ice*
When we sing about
Eating all your rice.

I told you **twice**.
It isn't very **nice**.
And you'll pay the **price**
If you don't eat your **rice**.
It isn't very **nice**
To leave it for the **mice**.
You'll pay the **price**
If you don't eat your
   rice.

Now remember, the
   letters i-c-e
Always say *ice*
Just think of the story
About eating all your
   rice.

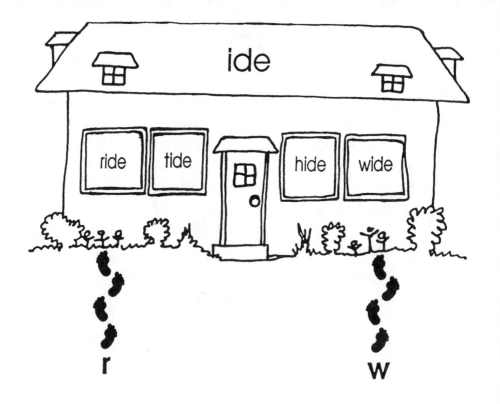

ide

ride tide hide wide

r w

* *

Follow the path to make words in the **ide** family. Write the word on the line.

sl ide

h ide

- 20 -

IDE

The letters i-d-e,
They always say *ide*
Just like in the words
Ride and side,
Wide and hide,
And slide and pride.

The letters i-d-e,
They always say *ide*.

R says *r*.
Put *r* before *ide*.
R-ide always says ride.

S says *s*.
Put *s* before *ide*.
S-ide always says side.

Well, t says *t*.
Put *t* before *ide*.
T-ide always says tide.

Now let's use
Some of these new words
In a silly song
That you have never
   heard.

Before I take a ride
On the water slide,
I will try to hide
In the shed outside.
And watch the ocean
   wide

Bringing in the highest
   tide.
I'll be filled
   with pride
Just before I
   take my
   ride.

Now YOU can say
The words with *ide*
When we sing about
Taking a ride.

Before I take a **ride**
On the water **slide**,
I will try to **hide**
In the shed **outside**.
And watch the ocean
   wide
Bringing in the highest
   tide.
I'll be filled with **pride**
Just before I take my **ride**.

Now remember, the let-
   ters i-d-e
Always say *ide*
Just think of the story
About taking a ride.

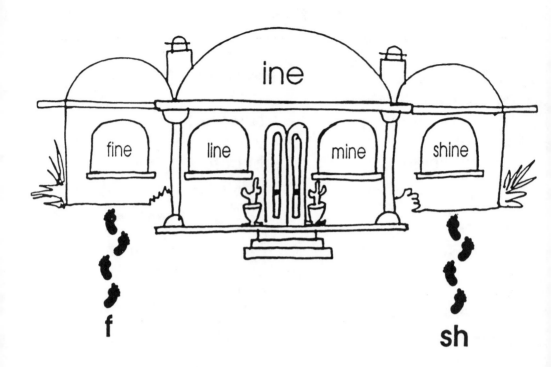

****

Follow the path to make words in the **ine** family. Write the word on the line.

v  /ine

_____

p  ine

_____

- 22 -

INE

The letters i-n-e,
They always say *ine*.
Just like in the words
Fine and mine,
Nine and shine,
And pine and line.

The letters i-n-e,
They always say *ine*.

L says *l*.
Put l before *ine*.
L-ine always says line.

P says *p*.
Put p before *ine*.
P-ine always says pine.

Well, f says *f*.
Put f before *ine*.
F-ine always says fine.

Now let's use
Some of these new words,
In a silly song
That you have never
  heard.

Won't it be fine
When all the candy's
  mine.
I will stand in line
In the bright sunshine.
If I have to wait 'till nine
In that long hot line.

It will be so fine
When all the candy's
  mine.

Now YOU can say
The words with *ine*
When we sing
All the candy's mine.

Won't it be **fine**
When all the candy's
  mine.
I will stand in **line**
In the bright **sunshine.**
If I have to wait till **nine**
In that long hot **line**
It will be so **fine**
When all the candy's
  mine.

Now remember, the
  letters i-n-e
Always say *ine*
Just think of the story
When all the candy's
  mine.

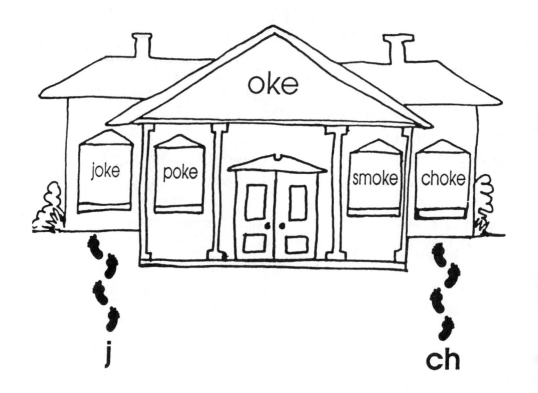

****

Follow the path to make words in the **oke** family. Write the word on the line.

j `oke`

_____

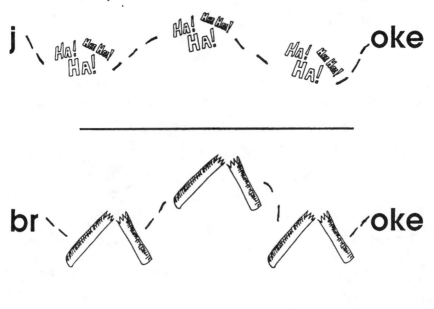

br `oke`

_____

OKE

The letters o-k-e,
They always say *oke*
Just like in the words
Joke and choke,
Smoke and stroke,
And spoke and poke.

The letters o-k-e,
They always say *oke*.

J says *j*.
Put *j* before *oke*
J-oke always says joke.

P says *p*.
Put *p* before *oke*.
P-oke always says poke.

Well c-h says *ch*.
Put *ch* before *oke*.
Ch-oke always says
    choke.

Now let's use
Some of these new words
In a silly song that
You have never heard.

If you ever smoke
You are sure to choke.
Or to have a stroke
And then to go broke.
And there's no joke
In a stroke or choke.

So don't
    you
    ever
    smoke
No...never
    ever
    smoke.

Now YOU
    can say
The words
    with *oke*
When we
    sing
About never ever smoke.

If you ever **smoke**
You are sure to **choke**.
Or to have a **stroke** ,
And then to go **broke**
And there's no **joke**
In a stroke or **choke**.
So don't you ever **smoke**
No...never ever **smoke.**

Now remember, the let-
    ters o-k-e
Always say *oke*
Just think of the story
And never ever smoke.

- 25 -

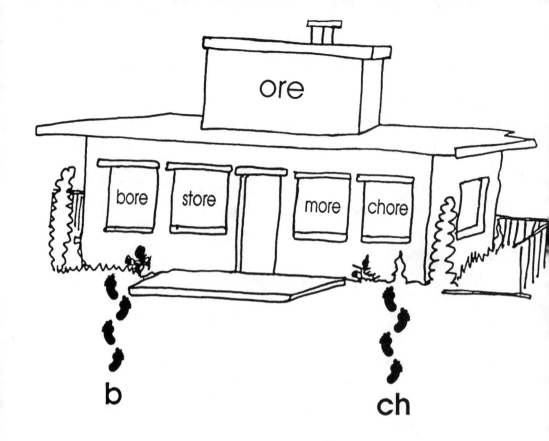

ore

bore   store   more   chore

b   ch

* *

Follow the path to make words in the **ore** family. Write the word on the line.

st ___ ore

_____

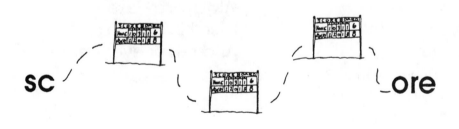

sc ___ ore

_____

ORE

The letters o-r-e,
They always say *ore*.
Just like in the words
More and chore,
Bore and store,
And core and score.

The letters o-r-e,
They always say *ore*.

M says *m*.
Put *m* before *ore*.
M-*ore* always says more.

B says *b*.
Put *b* before *ore*.
B-*ore* always says bore.

Well c says *c*.
Put *c* before *ore*.
C-*ore* always says core.

Now let's use
Some of these new words
In a silly song that
You have never heard.

I want more
Of what I adore.
But it's such a bore,
To go to the store.
So I'll just ignore
My list of chores.
And I won't get more

Of what I adore.

Now YOU can say
The words with *ore*
When we sing about
What I adore.

I want **more**
Of what I **adore.**
But it's such a **bore,**
To go to the **store.**
So I'll just **ignore**
My list of **chores.**
And I won't get **more**
Of what I **adore.**

Now remember, the let-
   ters o-r-e
Always say *ore*,
Just think of the story
About what I adore.

Collect other KIDZUP titles:

Grammar & Punctuation Songs
Phonics Songs, Short Vowels
Spelling Songs
Multiplication Songs
Addition Songs
ABC Songs
Colors, Shapes & Sizes

Any Questions? **1-888-321-KIDS**
Visit our award winning web site
www.kidzup.com